Walt Disney's

Cinderella

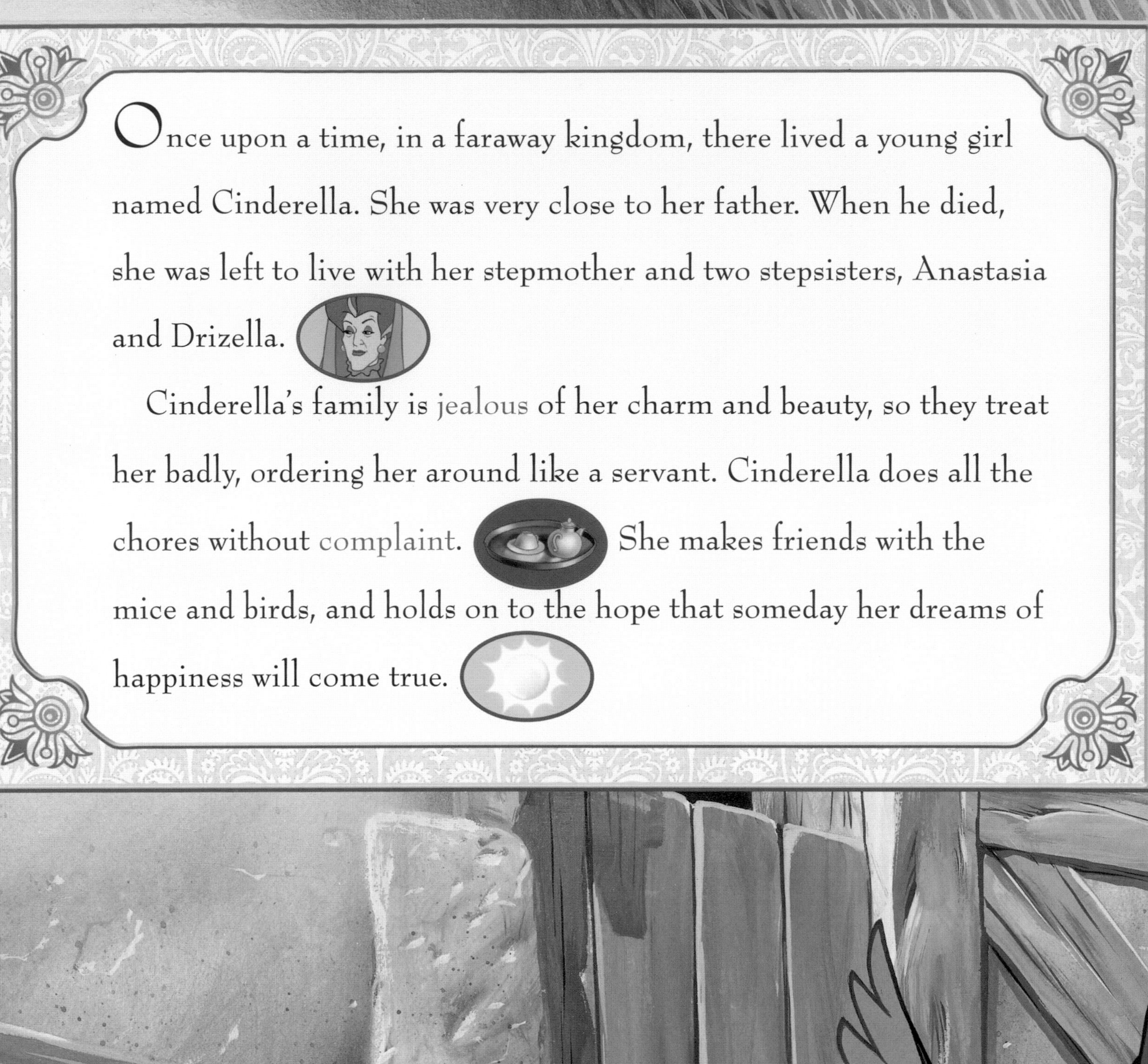

Once upon a time, in a faraway kingdom, there lived a young girl named Cinderella. She was very close to her father. When he died, she was left to live with her stepmother and two stepsisters, Anastasia and Drizella.

Cinderella's family is jealous of her charm and beauty, so they treat her badly, ordering her around like a servant. Cinderella does all the chores without complaint. She makes friends with the mice and birds, and holds on to the hope that someday her dreams of happiness will come true.

One day, a messenger arrives at the house with an envelope. Inside is an important invitation from the palace.

The King is throwing a ball in honor of his son, the Prince. By royal command, every maiden is to attend the ball.

"Why, that means I can go too!" says Cinderella excitedly.

Anastasia and Drizella laugh at Cinderella. Cinderella's stepmother tells her that she may go to the ball only *if* she finishes her chores and has something suitable to wear.

Cinderella runs to her room to fix a dress that belonged to her mother. Before Cinderella can even begin, her stepmother gives her more chores to do.

"Poor Cinderelly," says Jaq. He knows she'll never get her dress done.

The mice and birds decide to surprise Cinderella. They gather discarded objects from around the house and create a beautiful dress. Cinderella is delighted and thanks her friends for their thoughtfulness!

Cinderella's family is surprised when she rushes downstairs ready for the ball. Drizella and Anastasia are jealous. They accuse Cinderella of using their things to make her dress. Then, they rip the items off the dress. Cinderella's ball gown is ruined!

"Goodnight," the Stepmother says, smiling as she and her daughters leave for the ball.

Cinderella runs into the garden and weeps.

Suddenly, her fairy godmother appears. "Dry those tears," she says kindly. "You can't go to the ball looking like that."

With her magic wand, the Fairy Godmother changes a pumpkin into a carriage. She also transforms Cinderella from head to toe.

"Oh, it's a beautiful dress," says Cinderella. "And look — glass slippers!"

The Fairy Godmother also tranforms Cinderella's friends. They will help take Cinderella to the ball.

The Fairy Godmother wishes Cinderella well and warns her that the magic will not last past midnight. "On the stroke of twelve," she says, "the spell will be broken."

With that, Cinderella and her friends depart for the royal ball.

When Cinderella arrives at the ball, she meets a handsome man, but she does not know he is the Prince.

The Prince and Cinderella dance together all evening. They are enchanted with one another.

"Who is this beautiful woman?" everyone wonders.

Cinderella enjoys herself so much, she completely forgets about the time. Suddenly, she hears a clock strike midnight! She remembers her fairy godmother's warning.

"Oh my goodness," she says, pulling away from the Prince. "It's midnight!"

"No, wait!" the Prince replies.

Time

Cinderella runs down the palace steps.

"Come back!" the Prince calls out. "I don't even know your name!"

Cinderella loses a glass slipper, but is in too much of a hurry to stop. The Prince finds the lone slipper on the staircase as Cinderella disappears into the night.

Cinderella makes it safely to her carriage. As it pulls away from the palace, the last stroke of midnight chimes. The magic wears off. Everything is as it was before — except for a single glass slipper.

The slipper will serve as a souvenir for Cinderella of this special evening. "Thank you so much," Cinderella whispers as she thinks of her fairy godmother.

Magic

The next morning, the Prince announces he will marry the woman from the ball. The King sends the Grand Duke out to find the maiden whose foot fits the glass slipper. Every girl will get to try the slipper on!

The Stepmother locks Cinderella in her room. She instructs Anastasia and Drizella to pretend the slipper fits them. "If one can be found whom the slipper fits, then by the King's command, that girl shall be the Prince's bride."

The Grand Duke arrives with his footman.

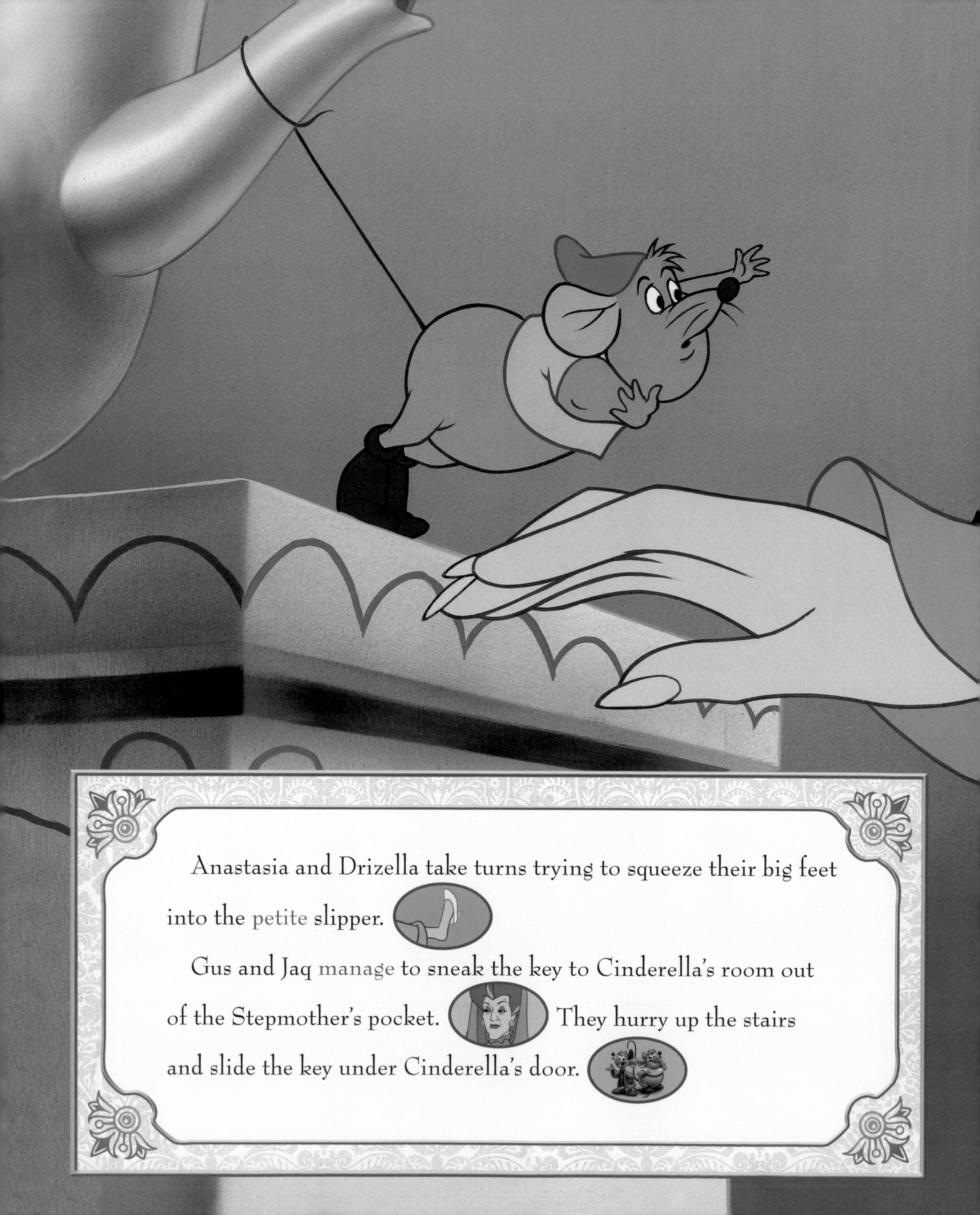

Anastasia and Drizella take turns trying to squeeze their big feet into the petite slipper.

Gus and Jaq manage to sneak the key to Cinderella's room out of the Stepmother's pocket. They hurry up the stairs and slide the key under Cinderella's door.

Maze

Just as the Grand Duke is about to exit with the slipper, Cinderella appears.

"Your Grace!" she cries out. "May I try it on?"

The Grand Duke nods. The Stepmother sticks out her cane and trips the footman carrying the slipper. He drops it and the slipper breaks!

"Oh no!" the Grand Duke cries.

"Perhaps, if it would help," suggests Cinderella. She pulls the matching slipper from her pocket and easily slips it onto her foot.

Shoes